About the author

Working for many years in nature conservation, recognisi
time absorbed in nature and truly noticing it leads to a true relationship with the natural world, is the reason Katherine began to write **The Adventures of Wildwell Hollow**; that and her love of fairies and the discovery that bodkins do exist!

www.fiandbooks.com

First published in UK in 2021 by Fiona Woodhead from FiandBooks.com
67 The Hollins, Triangle, Halifax, West Yorkshire. HX6 3LU.
www.fiandbooks.com

Tilly Fairy & Bodkin Jack's fact file

- Red deer are native to the UK.
- Male red deer are known as stags, females are hinds and their young are calves.
- A monarch is a stag with 16 or more 'tines' or points on his antlers.
- A group of hinds gathered by a stag is a harem.
- The sound a stag makes is a bellow or roar.
- Parallel walking enables two rival stags to size each other up, to assess their size and strength.
- Clashing antlers may happen when two stags fight, sometimes becoming 'locked' together.
- Stags often root through vegetation to mark their territory, resulting in decorated antlers when vegetation gets caught up on the tines.
- Bolving competitions are a real thing! Look them up on You Tube.
- The rutting season is when stags and hinds come together to mate.
- Emotions run high during the rut so you don't want to get in the way! Make sure you watch from a safe distance.

Love Tilly Fairy and Bodkin Jack

xxx

Wildwell Hollow

Wild Adventure Badge

Carried by the crisp autumn breeze, the eerie call of the moorland beast crept through the keyhole of Toadstool Cottage.

Tilly Fairy threw back her patchwork blanket, bounced out of bed and flung open the window. The sun filled the room with comforting warmth.

It was going to be an exciting day in Wildwell Hollow!

...ROOOAAARRRR...

Toadstool Cottage

Bodkin Jack must already be up, thought Tilly Fairy as wood-smoke danced past her window. There were few days when the elf-like bodkin didn't light the fire before breakfast in Tree Stump House. Tilly Fairy pulled on her lace-up boots over her newly knitted autumn socks. One sock was orange and the other was purple; she never wore two socks the same!

The woodland clearing was silent but for the birds gossiping in the trees high above. Tilly Fairy knocked with a rat-a-tat-tat on the bright red wooden door of Tree Stump House, and Bodkin Jack burst out shouting, "Hey hey, let's go!"

Tree Stump House

As the friends raced through Whispering Wood, nestled deep in Wildwell Hollow, the frosty red and orange leaves crunched underfoot. Tilly Fairy and Bodkin Jack could hear the rumbling roar on the moor in the distance.

"That's one big beast!" shrieked Tilly Fairy.

Bodkin Jack cupped his hands around his mouth, drew a deep breath and roared, "Not as big as me!"

Stick antlers

Handy rucksack

"If you're going to persuade the deer that you're the King of Stags, you'll need an impressive set of antlers," giggled Tilly Fairy.

The two friends set about making antlers out of twigs from the woodland floor.

They decorated them with autumn leaves tied on with string from Bodkin Jack's handy rucksack, which was always full of just the right things.

"Now we're ready," announced Tilly Fairy, as they threaded their handsomely decorated antlers into their hats and headdress, making them stand proud.

...ROOAARRRR...

Male red deer

Tilly Fairy fluttered her wings above Bodkin Jack as they raced over Brimstone Bridge, crossing the fresh cheerful waters of Babbling Brook.

The glowing sun was slowly melting away the night's frost. Their cheeks flushed bright and rosy as they climbed the heather clad hills of Monarch Moor that now held only a hint of purple.

...ROOOAAARRRR...

Suddenly, in the distance against a brilliant blue sky, stood the most majestic of creatures. Throwing back his head, steam rising from his mouth, a mighty roar bellowed from the depths of the red deer stag's throat. The haunting sound echoed across the moor telling all those who dared challenge him, that he was the mightiest stag of all.

"The King of Stags!" cried Bodkin Jack as they stared in wonder at the magnificent creature. Strutting with confidence and bellowing at his competitors, the King of Stags was indeed, the greatest beast by far.

Tilly Fairy and Bodkin Jack picked their way across the moor to Jumble Rocks. It was the middle of the rutting season, when all the male stags compete to win the admiration of the female hinds. There was never a dull moment on the moor!

Perched on a rock, Bodkin Jack slurped from his flask of steaming tea and munched his way through one of Tilly Fairy's homemade apple muffins. Tilly Fairy, too excited to eat, peered eagerly through her binoculars watching the drama unfold.

The King of Stags was an old gent with a glorious set of antlers. He was surrounded by an impressive group of hinds, their red coats glowing in the newly risen sun.

"Look how many hinds he has!" exclaimed Bodkin Jack bouncing with excitement. "When he wins the attention of a hind, she joins his harem," he explained.

"A harem of hinds!" giggled Tilly Fairy. "The King has the biggest harem on the moor!"

harem of hinds

As the noble old King became weary, younger, fitter stags attempted to steal his hinds, so far with little success. Suddenly, a new competitor emerged. With antlers held high, the young stag strutted towards the King.

The new challenger tasted the air on his tongue, threw back his head and bellowed, showing the hinds that he was well worth a second look.

The King stood his ground looking unimpressed and bellowed back with an almighty "ROOOAR!"

decorated antlers

Bodkin Jack and Tilly Fairy gawped as the two stags began walking alongside each other, sizing one another up. The hinds began making their choices and a few ran from the King's harem to the challenger's growing group.

"Oh no they're going to fight!" exclaimed Tilly Fairy, fluttering her wings nervously.

An almighty clash filled the air as antlers collided and the two stags fought to push the other out of the fight.

Before long, the young challenger realised his mistake.

Feeling the power and experience of the King, he reluctantly fled.

"Wow, he really is the King of Stags!" exclaimed Bodkin Jack jumping for joy.

"I reckon if we were both stags, I would win," challenged Tilly Fairy with her wings stretched wide.

"Ha! I accept your challenge. But if a stag roars or bellows, what does a bodkin and a fairy do?"

"Hmm, a roar, a bellow and...a BOLVƎ! A bolving bodkin!" chuckled Tilly Fairy.

The friends cupped their hands around their mouths and bolved with all their might, "ROOAAR!"

On the horizon, the King of Stags slowly turned to listen.

The powerful beast threw back his head and let out a menacing reply, "ROOOAAAR!"

...ROOOAAARRRR...

Frantically stumbling and tumbling, Bodkin Jack raced across the moor whilst Tilly Fairy flew at high speed above, finally landing by Babbling Brook.

"Your wings have never fluttered so fast," puffed Bodkin Jack.

"I wasn't waiting for the King to decide whether I was worth a fight!" gasped Tilly Fairy.

That evening, back in Whispering Wood, Tilly Fairy and Bodkin Jack sat around a glowing campfire with their friends and told stories of their wild adventure.

In the flickering firelight the bodkins and fairies played out the day's events.

They strutted alongside one another, sizing each other up. Competed in a game of tug of war, using their strength to win the battle. Wore decorated antlers and took turns to challenge each other to bellow and bolve.

Meanwhile, over the crackling fire and high above the Whispering Wood, a distant echo of the King of Stags rumbled on.

Now, each year when the autumn leaves are falling and the red deer stags are roaring, the bodkins and fairies stand side by side at the edge of Whispering Wood for the annual Fairy and Bodkin Bolve Off.

One by one they throw back their heads, puff out their chests and roar, tempting the King of Stags to return their challenge with the most impressive roar on the moor!